AMERICAN TALL TALES

Johnny Appleseed

D1497212

Retold by M. J. York ❧ Illustrated by Michael Garland

The Child's World®
1980 Lookout Drive • Mankato, MN 56003-1705
800-599-READ • www.childsworld.com

Acknowledgments
The Child's World®: Mary Berendes, Publishing Director
The Design Lab: Kathleen Petelinsek, Design
Red Line Editorial: Editorial direction

Copyright © 2013 by The Child's World®
All rights reserved. No part of this book may be reproduced or utilized in
any form or by any means without written permission from the publisher.

ISBN 9781614732105
LCCN 2012932260

Printed in the United States of America
Mankato, MN
January 2013
PA02166

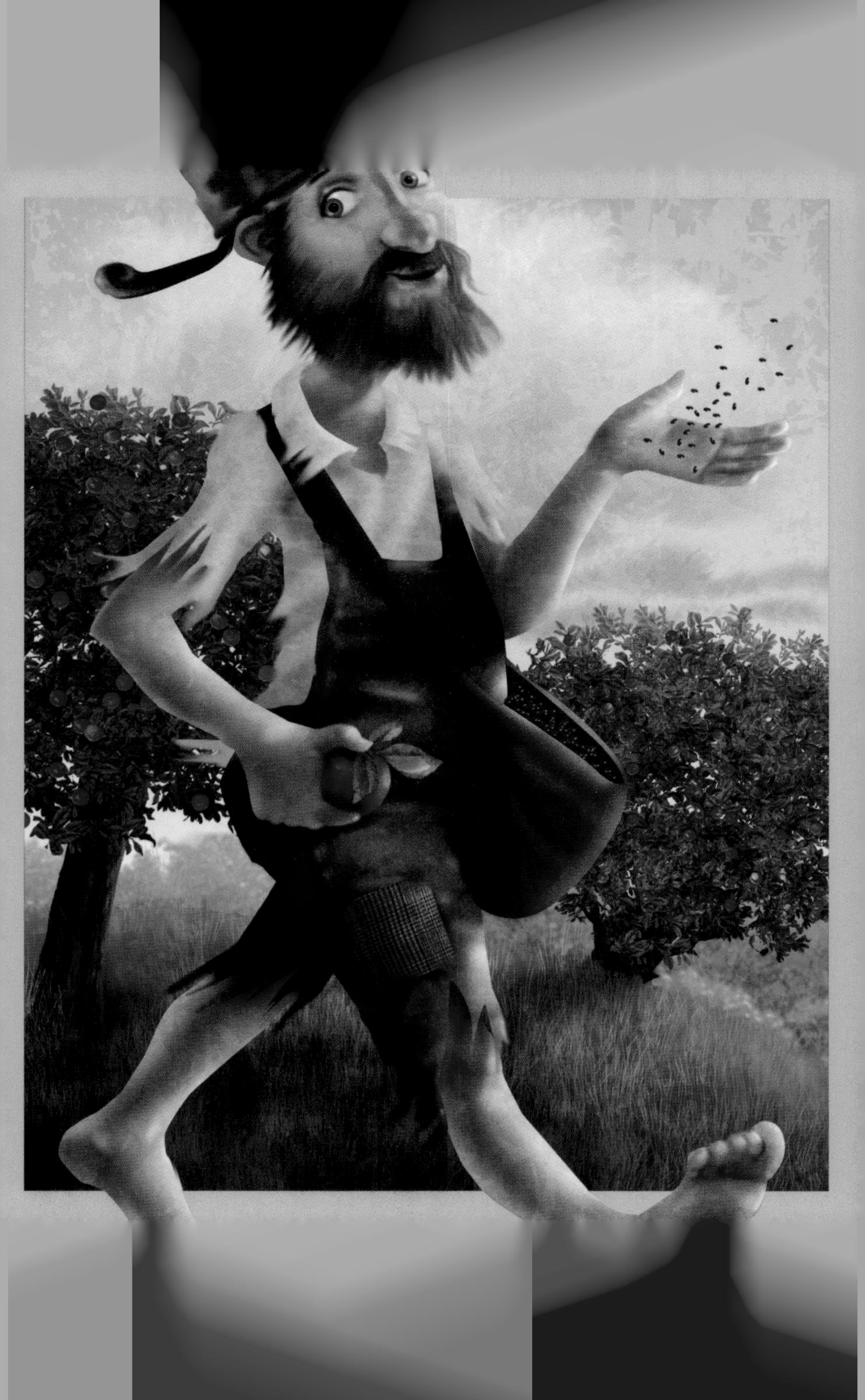

Long, long ago, a wee baby was born in Massachusetts and given the name John Chapman. In those days, most Americans lived on the East Coast, and they were only beginning to move west into Ohio, Pennsylvania, and Indiana. You might ask why we still remember humble John Chapman even today. He did not lead armies into battle or run the government. He did not found a city or invent something important.

No, we remember John Chapman for something simpler, something smaller. And that something is part of his name. You've probably heard of him, too. His nickname was Johnny Appleseed.

Now, some people say Johnny Appleseed loved apples right from the start, while he was still a babe in his cradle. They say he would fuss and cry something spectacular until his mother fed him applesauce or gave him cider or brought him apple blossoms. That baby boy would giggle for hours watching the branches of an apple tree sway in the breeze.

When he grew a little older, an apple was his favorite ball for catching, and the branch of an apple tree was his favorite perch for daydreaming. He loved the other trees of the forest, too. His mother taught him the names of all the plants and animals. He loved the animals, and they loved

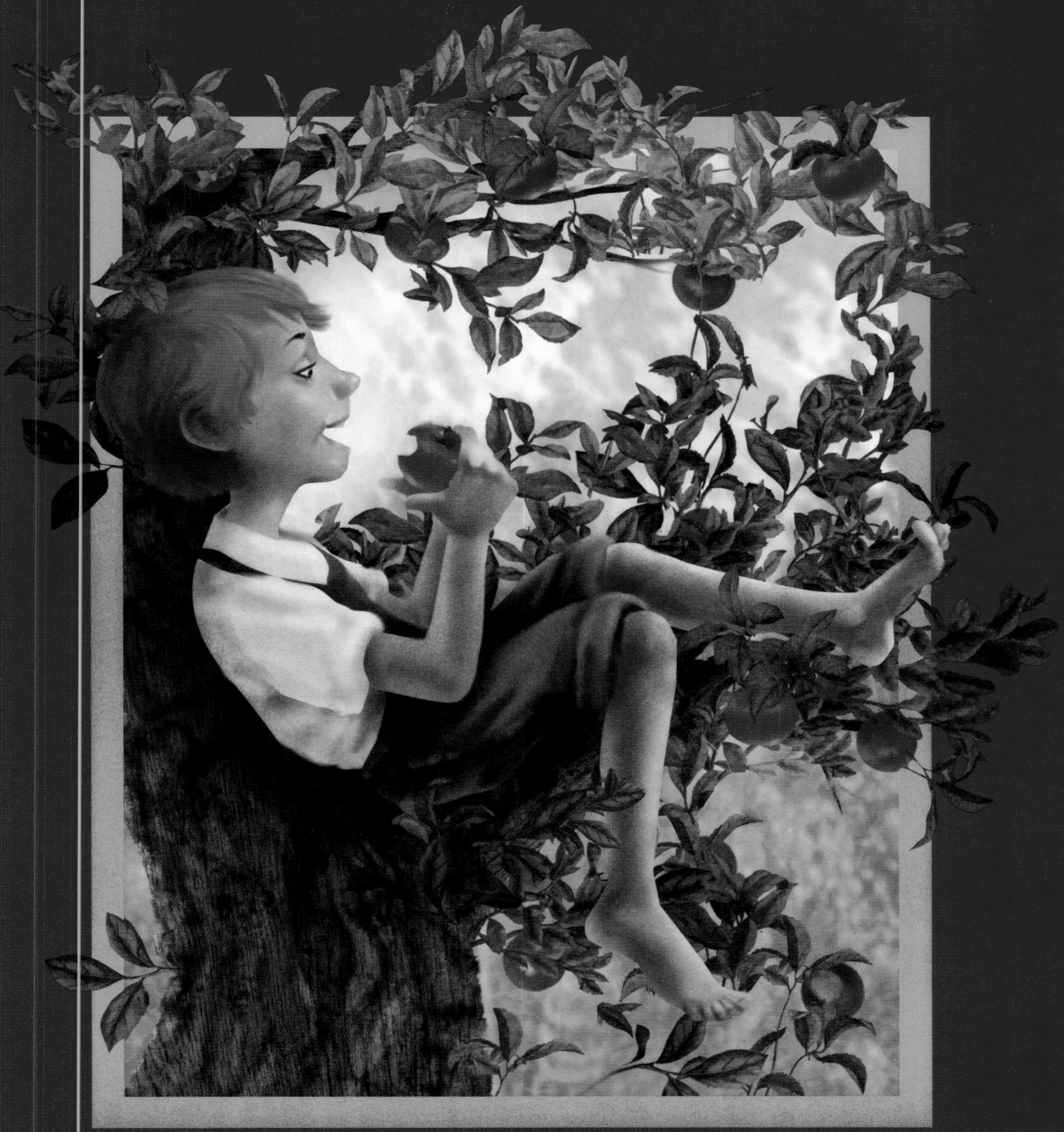

him right back. Does with their fawns would come up to lick his hand. Crows would bring him shiny bits and bobs they found by the sides of roads. And bears would lead him to the ripest berry patches.

When he had grown into a young man, Johnny's feet began to itch. You see, Johnny's itching feet were telling him it was time to leave home and see the world. But Johnny did not mean to merely wander. Oh, no, Johnny

Appleseed had a mission in mind when he was getting ready to leave home. He knew people were fast moving west. Where they were moving, though, there were no apple trees.

Johnny couldn't imagine a life without apples. He didn't want the pioneers in their new homes to be missing out on apple cider and applesauce and apple pies and apple turnovers and apple cake and— you get the idea.

So Johnny went and he gathered a big bag of apple seeds from the mill where they pressed apple cider. They had no use for the seeds at the mill, so they were happy to let Johnny take them.

Soon Johnny was ready to leave home. He had his bag of seeds, and he took a cooking pot so he could make dinner wherever he went. He carried the bag in his hand, but he wore the pot on his head where it made a fine hat.

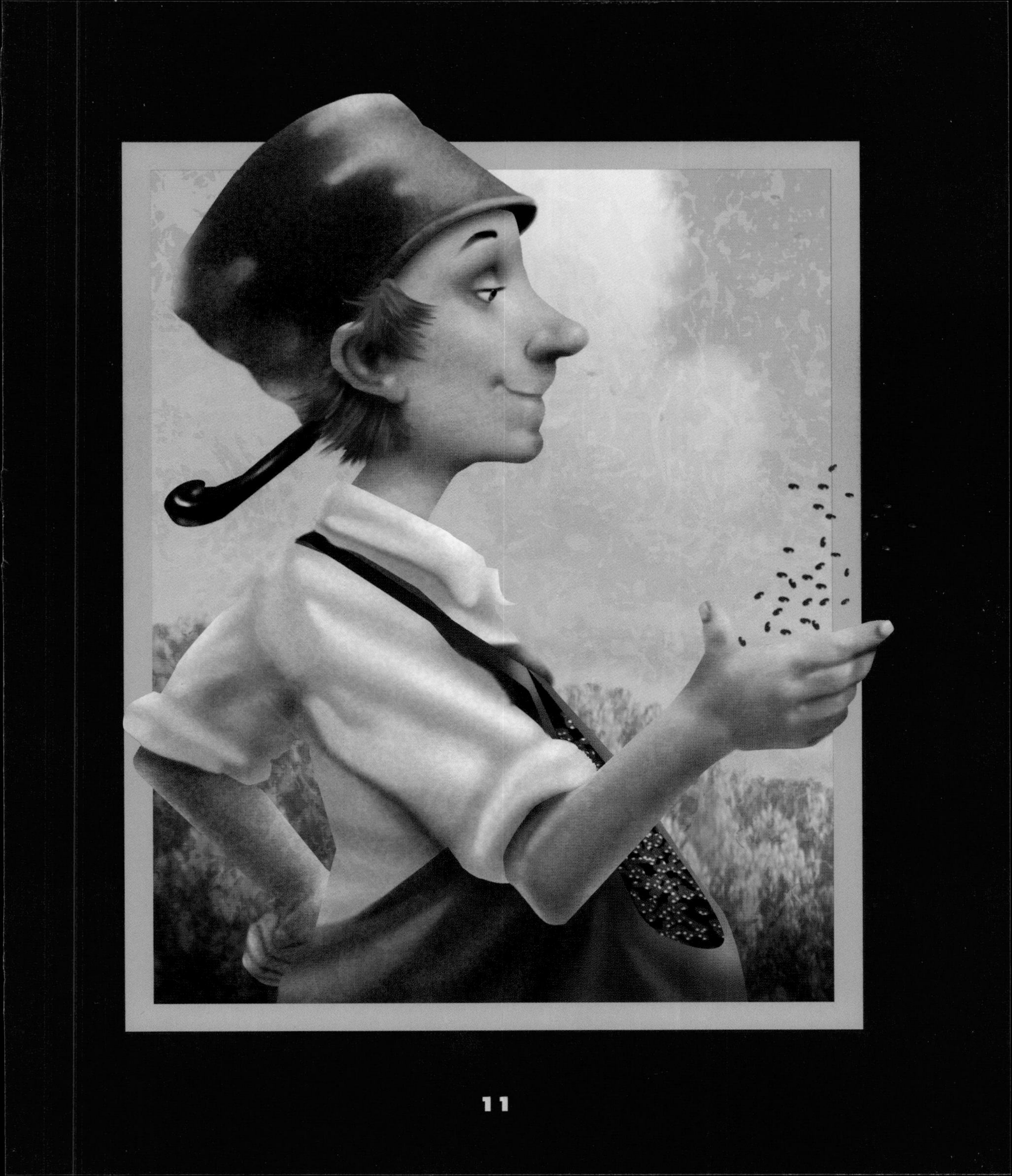

Johnny walked and he walked, walking circles through New York, Pennsylvania, Ohio, and Indiana. He walked through rain and he walked through snow. Sometimes he walked on roads and his journey was easy. Sometimes he pushed through tangled forests so thick, he must have been the first person to come through, ever. Johnny walked so far he wore his shoes clear off. The soles of his feet grew tougher than the toughest boots.

Johnny never wanted harm
to come to any animal. This
love of all life included even
the lowliest of creatures.
Why, one summer, he noticed
mosquitoes were flying into his
campfire and burning up. He
immediately put the fire out. He
didn't want to be comfortable if
it meant another creature dying.
If he was stung by a hornet, he'd
take it gently in his hands and
release it. He was once bit by
a rattlesnake and killed it by

accident. He felt sorry about it for years afterward.

One cold winter's night, Johnny went to curl up in an old hollow log. He planned to build a fire outside and curl up, snug as a bug. When he poked his nose in, however, he had a surprise. A mother bear and her two cubs had beaten him to the log. Quietly, so as to not disturb anybody, Johnny backed right out of the log and made his camp outside in the snow.

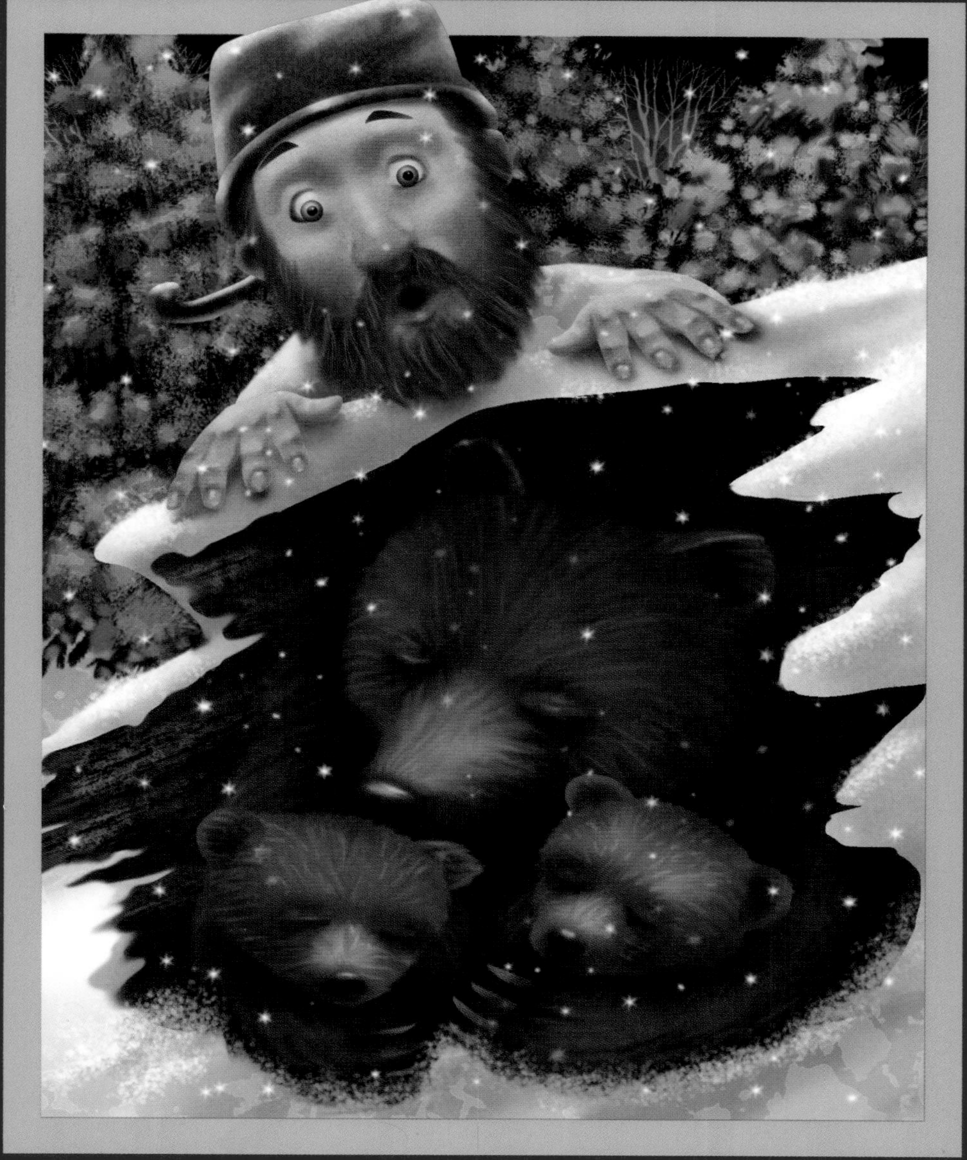

Johnny made friends everywhere he went. He made friends with farmers and pioneers. They often shared their supper with him, or else Johnny cooked up a fine stew for everybody in his cooking-pot hat. When Johnny's shirt or pants got ragged, one of his new friends would sew them up again. Some of his friends even gave him new clothes. And every time they said good-bye, Johnny left his friends with small sacks of apple seeds to plant on their own farms. Decades later, you could tell where Johnny Appleseed had been by the orchards that grew up behind him.

The longer Johnny walked, the less respectable he looked. At times, he wore nothing more

than a grain sack with a hole in the bottom for his head and a length of twine for his belt. But folks didn't mind. They knew old Johnny Appleseed was on a mission. He loved to stop and chat and tell his life story. Long after he'd walked on, Johnny's friends talked about how generous he was and about his kindness to animals. And he grew in their memories as the apple trees grew taller and stronger and bore loads of fruit.

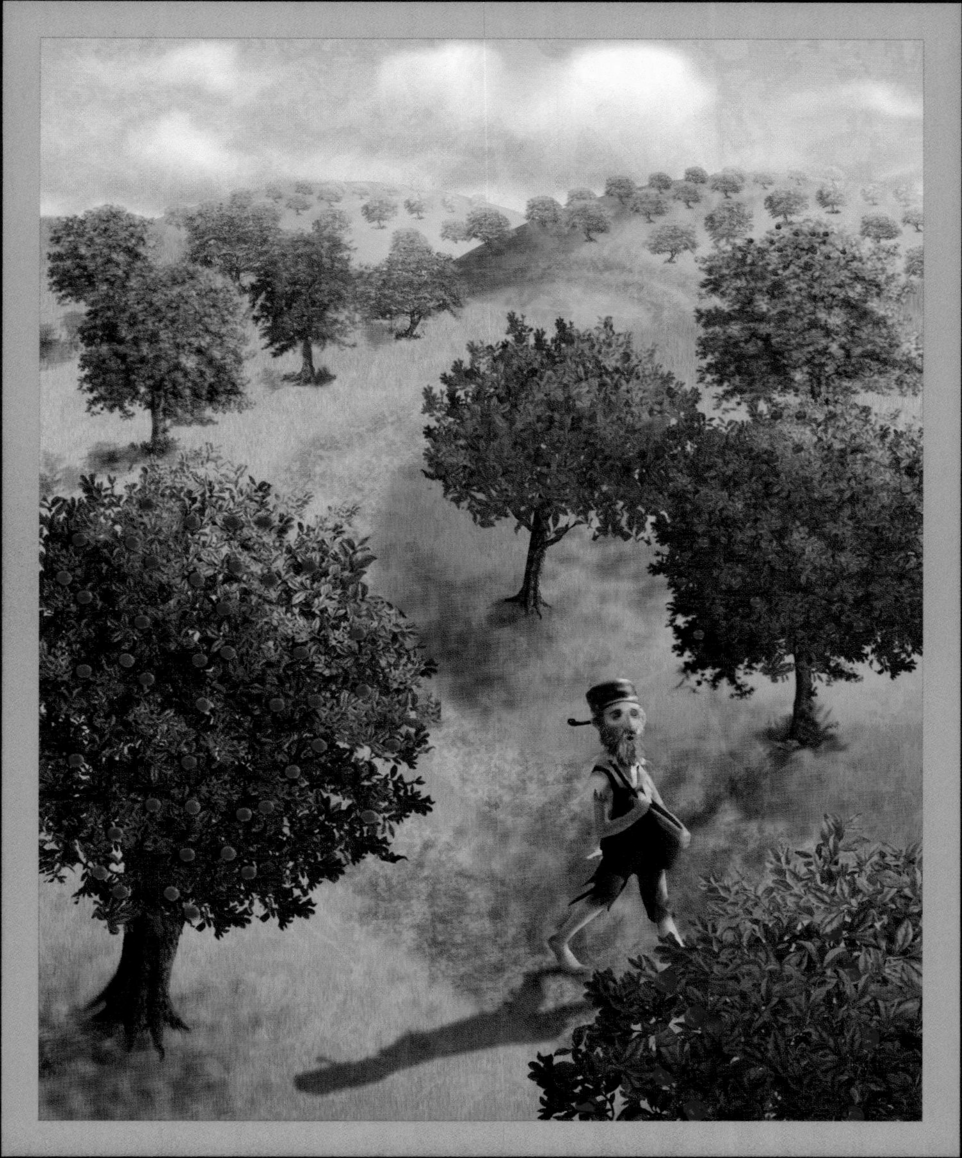

Johnny Appleseed walked
for years and years. Little girls
he'd brought ribbons became
grandmothers, and little boys
he'd carved wooden soldiers for
became old men. Then, one day,
Johnny Appleseed planted his
last tree. He lay down in one
of the first orchards he planted,
and he slept his last sleep.

Even today, if you go to the
right place in Ohio, throw your
head back and take a big sniff.
Did you catch a hint of apple

blossoms in the air? That's
the spirit of Johnny Appleseed
passing by.

BEYOND THE STORY

Have you ever told a true story but added in a few things to make it more exciting? That's what happens in the case of tall tales like *Johnny Appleseed*. Some people say tall tales started at bragging competitions of the old days. In trying to tell the best story, people would embellish and exaggerate fact. But many truths remain in tall tales, and in the case of *Johnny Appleseed*, such a man did exist.

John Chapman lived from 1774 to 1845. An American pioneer nurseryman, he introduced apple trees to many places, mostly in Ohio, Indiana, and Illinois. He became a legend because of his generosity and knowledge of cultivating land for apples.

We can only wonder if we would be eating so many apples today without Johnny's passion for sharing the fruit.

Johnny's legend as it's told in *Johnny Appleseed* also shows his kindness toward animals. He truly was a man that cared about nature and all its plants and creatures, even insects, they say.

Johnny Appleseed is a good example of the familiar, good-natured, often funny tone found in tall tales. When you read *Johnny Appleseed*, notice the narrator's language: "this here is the story," "what he did best was— well, you'll see." These words make us feel like we're being told the story from someone who was there. Because of that, it gives it an element of truth, or authenticity.

What parts of the Johnny Appleseed story do you believe? What parts do you think were made up?

ABOUT THE AUTHOR

M. J. York has an undergraduate degree in English and history and a master's degree in library science. M. J. lives in Minnesota and works as a children's book editor. She has always been fascinated by myths, legends, and fairy tales from around the world.

ABOUT THE ILLUSTRATOR

Michael Garland is a best-selling author and illustrator with thirty books to his credit. He has received numerous awards and his recent book, *Miss Smith and the Haunted Library*, made the New York Times Best Sellers list. Michael has illustrated for celebrity authors such as James Patterson and Gloria Estefan, and his book *Christmas Magic* has become a season classic. Michael lives in New York with his family.